THE CASE OF THE MYSTERIOUS MERMAID

Written by Vivian Binnamin
Illustrated by Jeffrey S. Nelsen

Silver Press

Library of Congress Cataloging-in-Publication Data

Library of Congress Cataloging-in-Publication Data
Binnamin, Vivian.
  The case of the mysterious mermaid / by Vivian
Binnamin; pictures by Jeffrey S. Nelsen.
      p.   cm.—(Field trip mysteries)
  Summary: On a class visit to the aquarium, Miss
Whimsy's fifteen students search for a missing mermaid.
  [1. Aquariums—Fiction.   2. Mystery and detective
stories.]   I. Nelsen, Jeffrey S., ill.   II. Title.   III. Series:
Binnamin, Vivian. Field trip mysteries.
PZ7.B51183Cat   [E]—dc20   89-24116
CIP   AC
ISBN 0-671-68817-0 (lib. bdg.)
ISBN 0-671-68821-9 (pbk.)

Published by Silver Press, a division of
Silver Burdett Press, Inc.,
Simon & Schuster, Inc.,
Prentice Hall Bldg., Englewood Cliffs, NJ 07632.
Printed in the United States of America.

10 9 8 7 6 5 4 3 2 1

Attention All Detectives!

Yes, you can be a detective, too, right along with Miss Whimsy and the Fantastic Fifteen. Just pay close attention to the story and the pictures in the book. There are clues hidden there, and the Fantastic Fifteen will be looking for them. See if you can discover them first!

Our teacher, Miss Whimsy, calls us the Fantastic Fifteen. And for good reason!

Miss Whimsy taught us to peek, poke, and prove. That's right. She solves mysteries. Miss Whimsy is a great detective. Now we're great detectives, too. That is a good thing, because wherever we go, mysteries seem to follow.

Miss Whimsy's
Third Grade

the

Fantastic
Fifteen

Miss Whimsy gave us each a different question. "Read your questions," said Miss Whimsy. "They may help you peek, poke, and prove at the City Aquarium today."

We already knew a thing or two about fish. After all, Raoul had two goldfish. Casey won a guppy at the fair last year. Gabe caught a sunfish in the lake. And Kate once ate lobster for dinner. But we never even heard of half the things in Miss Whimsy's questions!

As soon as we walked through the front doors, we saw a sign announcing the aquarium's birthday. The aquarium is just a little older than we are.

Inside there were streamers and fish balloons all over. A pudgy man was opening a tall wooden crate in the front hall.

"Hello, Mr. Cluely," said Miss Whimsy to our guide for the day. "Meet the Fantastic Fifteen."

We smiled.

"Mr. Cluely will show us around. By the way, Mr. Cluely, what's in the box?" asked Miss Whimsy.

"Argh!" he grunted. "Surprise birthday present for the aquarium, Miss Whimsy. All we know is that it's from Herbert Von Sherbet, the famous artist. I can't wait to see what's inside!"

We couldn't wait either. But Mr. Cluely warned us to stand back. "Anything can pounce out of a surprise birthday present!" he added.

After prying off the crate's side, Mr. Cluely found a note. He put on his glasses to read.

This marvelous mermaid is for the aquarium's birthday celebration. Now I'm off to Antarctica to look for hot spots in the cold continent.

Best wishes,

Herbert Von Sherbet

Famous Artist

Mr. Cluely tore away the wrapping paper. Inside was a lot of shredded paper. Mr. Cluely pushed that aside. Under the paper was plastic wrap. He peeled away the plastic. The package got smaller and smaller. We saw no present. We saw no mermaid. We saw nothing. The box was empty!

"Our marvelous mermaid!" said Mr. Cluely. "Gone, gone, gone! And so is Mr. Von Sherbet. By now he must be halfway to Antarctica!"

"Very fishy!" said Miss Whimsy. "Certainly a case for the Fantastic Fifteen!"

We looked at the empty box. We looked at sad Mr. Cluely. We knew we had a mystery on our hands. We were ready for the case of the mysterious mermaid.

"May we peek around the aquarium?" asked Gabe.
"Sure," said Mr. Cluely. "Follow me."

In the middle of the building was a huge aquarium tank. It held millions of gallons of seawater. There were smaller tanks around the outside walls.

We saw hatchet fish, swordfish, stingrays, and lantern fish. But no mermaid.

We saw sharks, tuna, octopus, and oarfish. But no mermaid.

We saw sea horses, sea cows, and sea cucumbers. But no mermaid.
We found the answers to Miss Whimsy's questions. But we found no marvelous mermaid.

SEA HORSE
The female sea horse lays eggs, but the male carrie them until they hatch.

SEA CUCUMBER
A sea cucumber is an animal lives on the bottom of the se

"Vanished! Without a trace! Before we even met!" moaned Mr. Cluely.

"Hold your sea horse," warned Raoul. "We haven't poked around yet."
     "Yes, poke. Poke by all means," whimpered Mr. Cluely.

We poked. We tried. We chatted. We spied.
We listened. We spotted. We searched. We plotted.
By the time Miss Whimsy called us back to her, we had it.

"We did it," said Casey. "We solved the case of the mysterious mermaid."

"Prove it!" said Miss Whimsy proudly.

"There were no mermaids in the aquarium of course," said Gabe, "because there is no such thing as a mermaid. Not in real life, at least. Years ago, sailors saw sea cows and thought they were mermaids. But were they ever wrong!"

Sea Cow

Mermaid

Gabe

"A famous artist like Herbert Von Sherbet wouldn't send an empty box," said Kate.

"And look at the 'postage due' mark," said Casey. "The box was probably held at the post office for days."

"Besides, Herbert Von Sherbet is off to Antarctica," added Raoul. "The whole continent is ice! He must have a great interest in the stuff."

"And most important," Raoul continued, "look at the wooden box. It's dripping!"

"So?" asked Mr. Cluely. "So what?"

"Think!" said Miss Whimsy.

"Herbert Von Sherbet carved you a mermaid sculpture," said Kate. "A sculpture made of ice!"

"The marvelous ice mermaid has melted to a puddle," said Gabe. "Sad, but true . . . a real muddle," said Miss Whimsy.

"Of course! You're right! Ah, how thrilling it would have been! An ice mermaid for the aquarium's birthday! How we'll miss her!" cried Mr. Cluely.

Miss Whimsy looked at us. Her face sparkled with an idea.

"Just give us paint, brushes, and tape, Mr. Cluely," said Miss Whimsy. "I'm sure we can make something special for the aquarium's birthday."

And that's just what we did. We may not be famous artists. But we certainly are fantastic. If you're not sure, just ask Miss Whimsy.